D1420753

To my sisters, Jean, Polly and Lisa   KH

For Katharine, with love and thanks for years of fun with Angelina   HC

VIKING/PUFFIN

Published by the Penguin Group
Penguin Books Ltd, 27 Wrights Lane, London W8 5TZ, England
Penguin Books USA Inc., 375 Hudson Street, New York, New York 10014, USA
Penguin Books Australia Ltd, Ringwood, Victoria, Australia
Penguin Books Canada Ltd, 10 Alcorn Avenue, Toronto, Ontario, Canada M4V 3B2
Penguin Books India (P) Ltd, 11 Community Centre, Panchsheel Park, New Delhi – 110 017, India
Penguin Books (NZ) Ltd, Cnr Rosedale and Airborne Roads, Albany, Auckland, New Zealand
Penguin Books (South Africa) (Pty) Ltd, 5 Watkins Street, Denver Ext 4, Johannesburg 2094, South Africa

On the World Wide Web at: www.penguin.com

Penguin Books Ltd, Registered Offices: Harmondsworth, Middlesex, England

First published by ABC, All Books for Children, a division of The All Children's Company Ltd, 1991
Published by Viking 2001
1 3 5 7 9 10 8 6 4 2
Published in Puffin Books 2001
1 3 5 7 9 10 8 6 4 2

Copyright © HIT Entertainment plc, 2001
Text copyright © Katharine Holabird, 1991
Illustrations copyright © Helen Craig, 1991

The moral right of the author and illustrator has been asserted

All rights reserved.
Without limiting the rights under copyright reserved above, no part of this publication may be reproduced, stored in or introduced into a retrieval system,
or transmitted, in any form or by any means (electronic, mechanical, photocopying, recording or otherwise), without the prior written permission
of both the copyright owner and the above publisher of this book

Printed in Italy by Printer Trento Srl

British Library Cataloguing in Publication Data
A CIP catalogue record for this book is available from the British Library

ISBN 0–670–91160–7 Hardback
ISBN 0–140–56868–9 Paperback

To find out more about Angelina, visit her web site at **www.angelinaballerina.com**

20063610

MORAY COUNCIL
LIBRARIES &
INFORMATION SERVICES

JA

Angelina's Baby Sister

Story by **Katharine Holabird** Illustrations by **Helen Craig**

VIKING
—
PUFFIN BOOKS

Angelina was so excited. Very soon there was going to be a new baby in the family! Angelina couldn't wait to be a big sister, and it was hard to think about anything else – even when Miss Lilly gave Angelina a beautiful china statue as a prize at ballet school.

"Perhaps you can make up a dance to welcome the baby," suggested Miss Lilly when Angelina thanked her. Angelina raced home to show her mother the lovely prize.

Angelina ran so fast that she almost bumped into Dr Tuttle as he was leaving. "Your mother is resting upstairs," he said, "and she has a surprise for you …"

Angelina leaped up the stairs and into the bedroom – and there were her parents, gazing lovingly at the newborn baby.

"Her name is Polly," said Mrs Mouseling happily. "Would you like to hold her?" Angelina couldn't believe how delicate her little sister was.

"I'll be a good big sister, Polly," Angelina said softly, as she rocked the baby in her arms.

Angelina's father smiled at her. "We know you will," he said.

That evening Angelina and her father made supper while Mrs Mouseling stayed in bed with Polly.

"Don't worry. Pretty soon your mother will be up and around again," said Angelina's father, "but now we have to take good care of her."

Angelina felt sad and confused. Why should one little baby need so much attention and make her mother feel so tired?

Angelina played with the pretty china dancer. Before she went to sleep she placed it carefully on her chest of draws where she could show it to her mother.

But the next day Angelina's mother was so busy looking
after the new baby that there was no time to look at
Angelina's prize, and the day after that Polly sneezed
several times and Dr Tuttle came back to see that she
didn't catch a cold.

Mr Mouseling was a good cook, but Angelina
missed her mother's special Cheddar cheese
pies after school. Having a baby sister
was not at all the way Angelina
had imagined it would be!

A whole week went by. Angelina
went to school every day and
tried to be good while
everyone fussed over
Polly, but it was
very hard.

The weekend came, and Angelina's grandparents arrived to visit. Angelina could hardly wait to see them again. When the doorbell rang she raced to answer it. "Grandma! Grandpa!" she shouted. "Just look at this!"

Angelina started to show her grandparents her new dance, but Grandma hugged Angelina quickly and said, "Wait just a minute, Angelina dear, first we have to see the baby!"

They went upstairs and Angelina could hear everyone laughing and talking together. She stamped her foot as loudly as she could, but nobody heard her. She tried to do a few steps of her dance but it seemed stupid and clumsy. Upstairs Grandpa was tickling Polly's toes.

"Isn't she just adorable!" Grandma exclaimed.

"Angelina – come and join us!" called her father. But Angelina didn't want to go and see Polly. At that moment she hated Polly and wished Polly would just disappear!

Angelina was so upset that she stomped to her room and slammed the door. Still nobody came. Angelina felt absolutely miserable. She was sure that nobody cared about her any more. Grandma and Grandpa didn't even want to see her dance!

Angelina grabbed one of her stuffed toys and threw it as hard as she could across the room, where it landed with a thud. Then she threw another and another. Angelina threw all of her stuffed toys and all of her dolls. Then she threw all her paper and crayons. She jumped up and down on her bed and she gave her chest of draws a terrific kick. The chest of draws shook, and down fell the china dancer, where it broke on the floor and lay in pieces.

"ANGELINA!"

Everyone was standing at the door. Angelina threw herself on her bed and burst into tears. Mrs Mouseling sat down on the bed and took Angelina in her arms.

"You were just as sweet as Polly when you were a baby," Angelina's mother smiled, "but now that you're bigger and we can do things together I love you more than ever."

"I just wanted to do my new dance and show
you my beautiful prize – but I got so angry I
broke it!" Angelina pointed at the broken china
dancer and cried even harder.

"I know someone who can fix it," said Mrs Mouseling,
and she gave the little figure to Grandpa,
who went off to get the glue.

"You promised to show us a dance,"
Grandma said, smiling, "and
we've been waiting all
this time."

Slowly Angelina began to feel better. "I guess it's not so
easy to get used to being a big sister," she admitted, wiping
her tears away. Grandma and Grandpa helped Angelina
pick up her toys and they all went downstairs for tea.

Mrs Mouseling had baked Angelina's favourite Cheddar cheese pies. "I wanted to surprise you," she said.

Then Mr Mouseling played his fiddle and Angelina did her special dance to welcome her baby sister, while Polly giggled with delight.

That night, Angelina showed Polly her favourite book, and helped put her to bed. "You know," she whispered, "when you get bigger I'm going to teach you to dance too!"

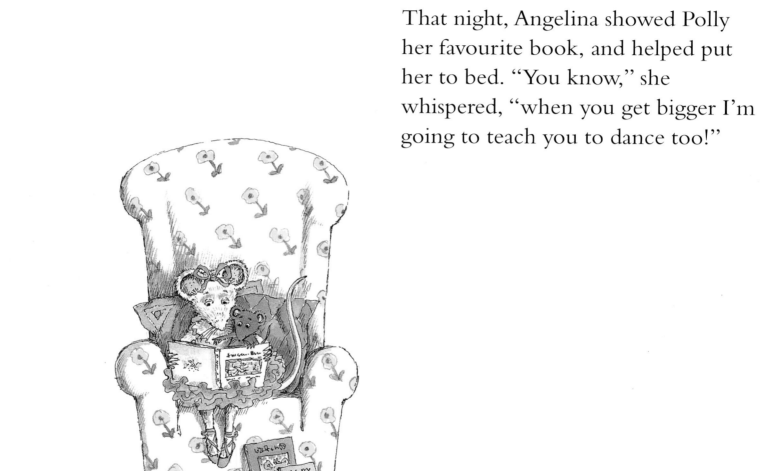